Disney's

Winnie the Pooh

Listen Up, Tigger

Pay attention!

That's the key

If there's a job to do.

Use your ears

And listen up

When people talk to you.

It was Christopher Robin's birthday. Pooh gathered all his friends together in the Hundred-Acre Wood to plan the perfect surprise party.

"We'll need someone to bring balloons, party hats, and oh, yes, the honey . . . ," Pooh said.

"Hoo-hoo-hoo! What can I do?" Tigger bounced up and down excitedly. "Stream the streamers? Toot the horns? I'm ready to spring-a-ding-ding into action. 'Cause springing is what tiggers do best!"

Rabbit frowned. “If you’d just stop bouncing around and listen,” he scolded.

“No problem, Buddy Boy,” said Tigger. “I’m listening!”

But as they went over the plans, Tigger fidgeted and fussed. He whirled and wiggled. He jiggled and wriggled. He hardly heard anything that was said.

While everyone was getting things ready for the party, Tigger was busy, too. He was busy bouncing and running around. Poor Tigger just couldn't sit still.

As Kanga and Roo worked hard to blow up balloons, Kanga asked Tigger to tie the balloons to the top of a tree. But instead, Tigger started to pop them. “How am I doin’ so far?” he asked.

"Tigger!" cried Kanga. "I said to tie the balloons to the TOP of that tree. Not POP them!"

"Sorry," Tigger apologized. "I'll listen harder next time."

Rabbit was busy baking a delicious honey birthday cake.

"Tigger, why don't you pour in the honey," Rabbit suggested. "Just a spot will do!" So Tigger poured in what he thought he heard—just a pot or two!

The honey flowed over the pot and all over the floor, making a big, sticky puddle right in the middle of Pooh's kitchen.

"Tigger! Why don't you pay attention?" Rabbit snapped.

"Oops," said Tigger. "I'll listen better next time!"

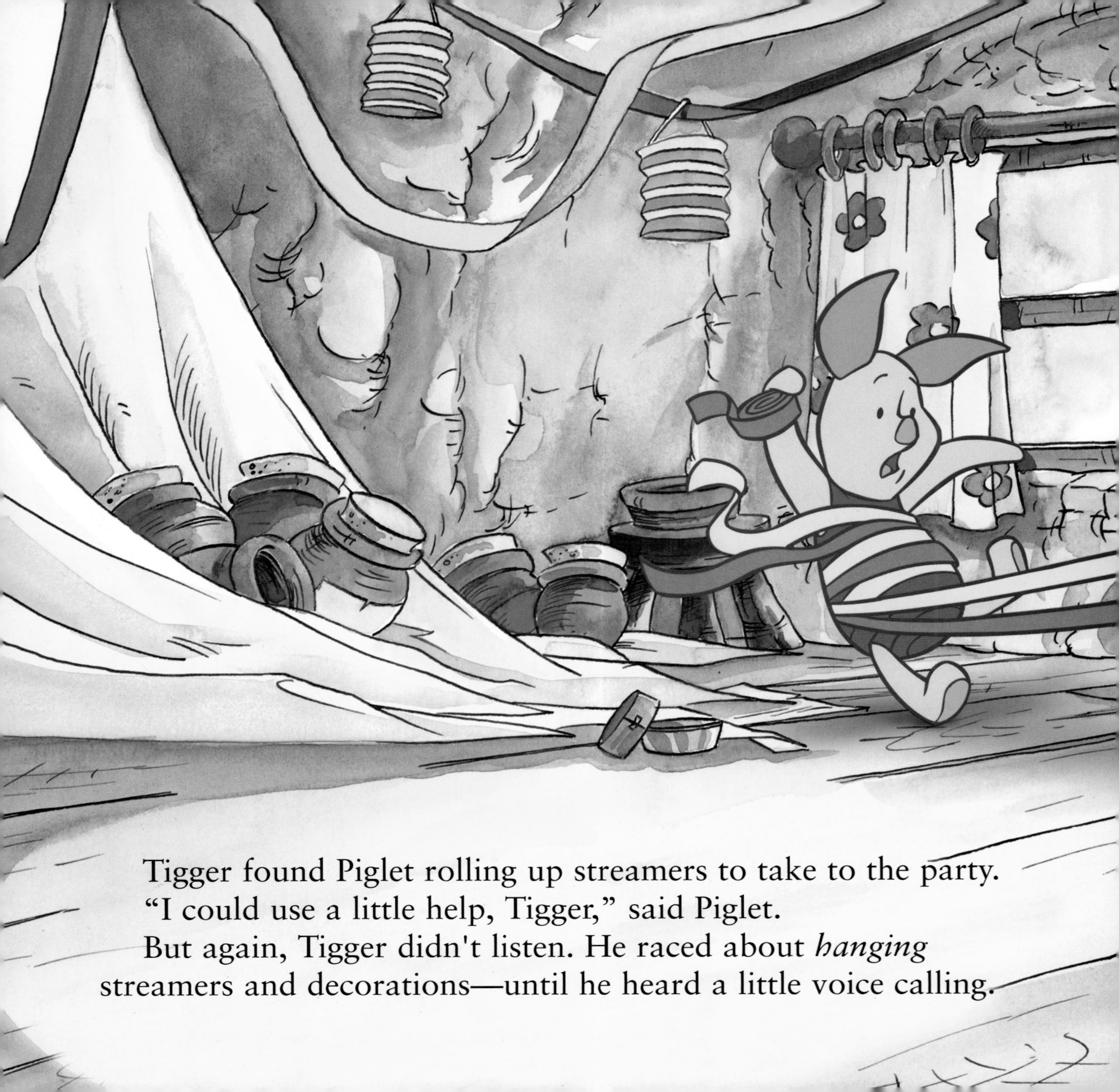

Tigger found Piglet rolling up streamers to take to the party.
"I could use a little help, Tigger," said Piglet.
But again, Tigger didn't listen. He raced about *hanging* streamers and decorations—until he heard a little voice calling.

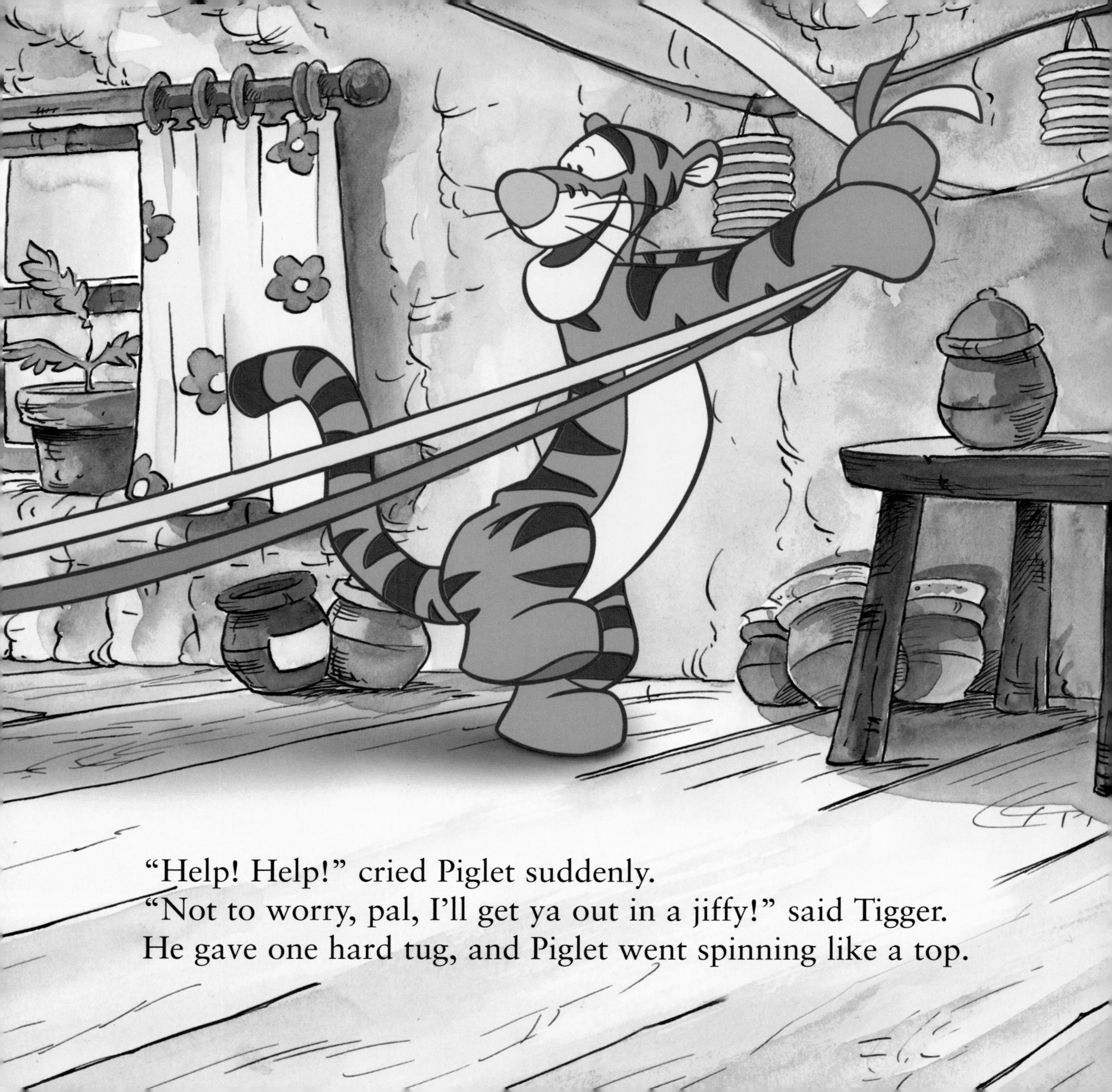

"Help! Help!" cried Piglet suddenly.
"Not to worry, pal, I'll get ya out in a jiffy!" said Tigger.
He gave one hard tug, and Piglet went spinning like a top.

And with that, Piglet crashed right into Pooh's table, where Eeyore and Owl had been gathering hats.

"I guess I must have missed a word or two of your directions," Tigger said. "Give me one more chance. I promise I'll listen!"

"Well, we do need someone to bring Christopher Robin to the secret spot in the Wood for his surprise party," said Owl.

"Secret missions are a tigger's specialty," Tigger explained. And with that, Tigger was off to get the guest of honor.

After all their hard work, everyone gathered for the party. The decorations were in place, and the birthday candles were lit. Everyone was hiding behind a big tree, ready to jump out and yell, "Surprise!"

“Mama, where do you suppose Christopher Robin is?” whispered Roo. “Tigger was supposed to bring him here.”

“Oh, dear. He is late,” sighed Kanga. “I hope Tigger paid attention to what we told him.”

But Tigger was having a hard time recalling exactly where the party was supposed to be. Was it at Piglet's or Pooh's? He took his best guess.

"This way," said Tigger, tugging on Christopher Robin's arm.

Tigger bounced through the door to Pooh's house and yelled, "Surprise!" But no one was there.

"What's going on, Tigger?" asked Christopher Robin.

"Follow me to Piglet's," said Tigger.

But Piglet's house was empty, too. And so was Kanga's.

"Gee, I must not have heard right," Tigger said to himself. "Where could the party be?"

"Where is everybody?" asked Christopher Robin. "Nobody seems to be home."

Tigger and Christopher Robin sat down to think.

Meanwhile, Pooh and his friends were getting worried.
“Maybe we should go look for them,” offered Kanga.
So off they went to search for Tigger and Christopher Robin.

"There you are, Pooh! We've been looking for you!" cried Christopher Robin, spotting his friend.

"But we've been looking for you," said Pooh. "This was supposed to be your surprise party."

“Aw, shucks. It’s all my fault,” said Tigger sadly. “I didn’t listen when I was told where the party was, and I ruined everything.”

“It’s okay, Tigger,” said Pooh. “There are still balloons and hats and games and birthday cake for everybody nearby.”

"And I think Tigger has learned an important lesson," said Owl. "Tigger has learned to listen."

"You bet I have!" Tigger agreed. "It's listen-listen-listen! Hoo-hoo!"

Christopher Robin thanked everybody, and then he made a wish before blowing out his candles.

“Sorry about the surprise,” Tigger said sincerely. “But from now on, pals o’ mine, I promise to be all ears.”

“And stripes, of course!” laughed Christopher Robin. “Because that’s what makes tiggers extra special.”

A LESSON A DAY POOH'S WAY

Always listen

before you leap

into action.